Book 2
short e

Phonics Reading Program

Out of the Nest

by Quinlan B. Lee

SCHOLASTIC INC.

New York Toronto London Auckland Sydney
Mexico City New Delhi Hong Kong Buenos Aires

The toucans need **help**!
They had four **eggs**
in their **nest**.
One, two, three.
Oh, no! An **egg fell** from
the **nest**!

Check next to those rocks.
Is there an **egg**? **Yes!**
Is it a toucan **egg**?
Let's check.

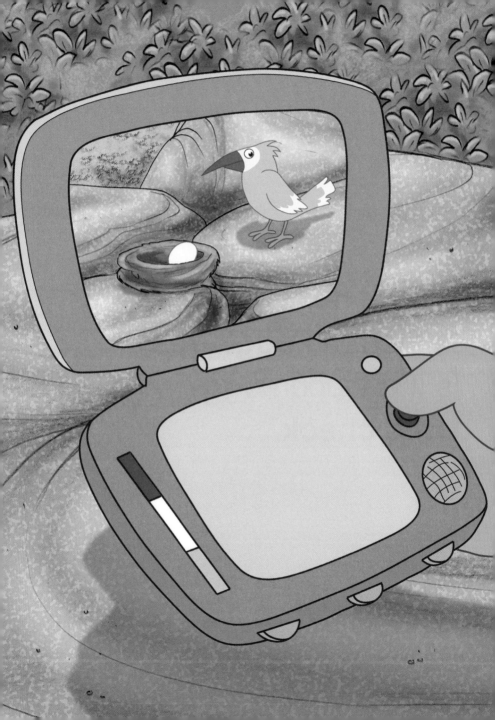

Toucans make **nests** in trees, not **next** to rocks. A **red**-billed tropic bird makes **nests next** to rocks. It is her **egg**.

Check next to the lake.
Is there an **egg**? **Yes!**
Is it a toucan **egg**?
Let's check!

Crocodiles make **nests** **next** to lakes.
This **egg** is a crocodile **egg**.
It is **best** to leave it alone.

There is another **egg**.
It is **next** to that tree.
Is it a toucan **egg**?
Let's check!

Yes! Toucans build **nests** in trees.

Toco, here is your **egg**. Now you can put it back in your **nest**.

We did it! Now the **eggs** are
in the **nest**.

Illustrated by Art Mawhinney
Designed by Kim Brown and Nancy Sabato

ISBN-13: 978-0-439-91306-5
ISBN-10: 0-439-91306-3

12 11 10 9 8 7 6 5 4 3 2 1   7 8 9 10 11/ 0

Printed in China
First printing, June 2007

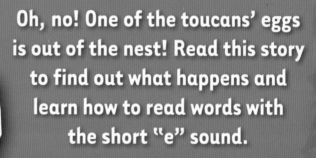

Oh, no! One of the toucans' eggs
is out of the nest! Read this story
to find out what happens and
learn how to read words with
the short "e" sound.

**Visit Diego anytime
at www.nickjr.com**

SCHOLASTIC

www.scholastic.com

ISBN-13: 978-0-439-91306-5
ISBN-10: 0-439-91306-3

EAN

9 780439 913065